A Different Land

Other Paul Jennings books published by Old Barn Books

A Different Dog
ISBN 9781910646427

The forest is dense and dark.
And the trail full of unexpected perils.
The dog can't move. The boy can't talk.
And you won't know why. Or where you are going.
You will put this story down
Not wanting the journey to end.

A Different Boy
ISBN 9781910646465

Longlisted for the CILIP Carnegie Medal 2019

The orphanage is far behind.
But life as a stowaway is even worse.
And nothing is what it seems on this sea of troubles.
Will Anton survive?
Can you guess the shocking truth?

It's a Paul Jennings story, so put on your life jacket –
your world might just capsize.

A Different Land

Paul JENNINGS

with illustrations by
Geoff KELLY

First published in Australia by Allen & Unwin in 2019
This UK edition first published by Old Barn Books Ltd 2019

Old Barn Books Ltd
Warren Barn
West Sussex
RH20 1JW

email: info@oldbarnbooks.com
web: www.oldbarnbooks.com
Distributed in the UK by Bounce Sales & Marketing Ltd
sales@bouncemarketing.co.uk

Teaching resources available from our website.

ISBN 9781910646496

Illustrations created with pen on paper and digitally drawn
Cover and text design by Sandra Nobes
Cover illustration by Geoff Kelly
Set in 12.5 Minion by Sandra Nobes
Printed in Denmark by Nørhaven

First UK edition
1 3 5 7 9 10 8 6 4 2

To Mary-Anne
with much love, Paul

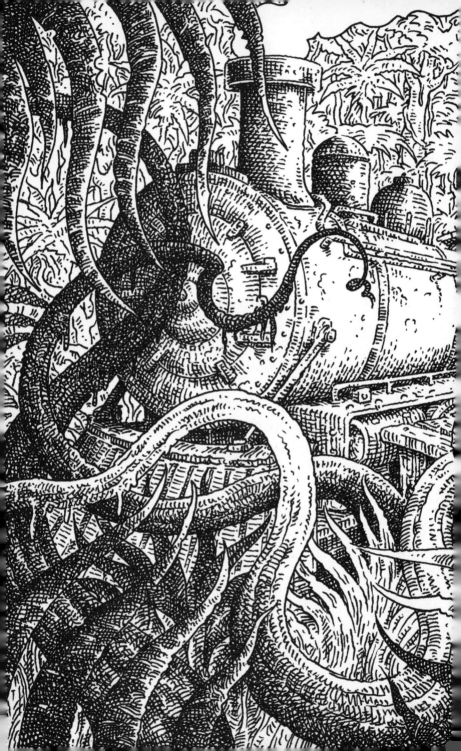

One

The three travellers stared around nervously. They were alone. And lonely. There had not been one other passenger on the last fifty miles of their journey in the little steam train.

The railway station, if you could call it that, was no more than a rotting platform struggling to compete with the encroaching vines and scrub.

The woman stared at the rusting hulk of a dead car that sat nearby in a tangle of creepers and ferns. Grass sprouted on its roof like damp hair. The surrounding rainforest was dark and steamy.

The only sign of life was a conductor unloading heavy sacks, tea chests and other goods out of the boxcar. He struggled to lift an iron anchor and dropped it with a clang.

A little beyond the platform, two forty-four-gallon drums marked the side of a dirt track that disappeared into the threatening mouth of the forest.

This was obviously the last stop. The railway tracks continued on for a short distance and then petered out, strangled by weeds and scrub. The taller of the two boys, the one with no hair, stared at them gloomily.

'I wonder where the tracks once ended,' he said.

'The end of the world,' answered the other boy.

'No, that's this place,' said his brother.

'Now, now, Christopher,' said the woman. 'Give it a chance.'

Christopher sighed. 'I thought someone was going to meet us,' he said. 'There's no sign of anyone.'

They all sat down on their cases and waited. Flies buzzed in the clammy heat.

Christopher rummaged in his pocket and pulled out a sausage wrapped in grease-proof paper. He waved it in front of his brother.

'Look what I've got, Anton,' he said cheekily. He smacked his lips and took a bite.

Anton suddenly grabbed it from Christopher's hand and held it over his head.

The boys began to fight for the sausage, laughing and jostling.

'Give it back, Anton,' said the woman.

'Okay, Pat,' he said.

Anton handed the sausage to their mother and she broke it into three. She gave them a section each and kept one for herself. She and Anton immediately began to chew, but Christopher wrapped his bit carefully.

The sausage brought back memories of a harder time. Images flashed through his mind. He remembered a land ravaged by war. A place of hunger and fear. He put his piece of sausage back in his pocket. Just in case. He looked at his mother and saw that she knew what he was thinking.

'It's all covered in fluff,' he said, trying to cover his thoughts. 'I'll keep it for emergencies.'

Anton looked around. 'There's not even a ticket office here,' he said.

'Or a toilet,' said Christopher. 'I need to pee.'

'In this country, you do it in the bushes,' said Anton. 'It's not like home.'

Christopher stepped down from the platform

and walked over to the rusty car. He climbed on the bonnet, did a little tap dance and bowed. Then he jumped down out of sight behind the vehicle.

Pat watched nervously. A minute passed. And then another.

'Snake, snake,' yelled Anton.

Christopher shot out from behind the car, trying to run and do up the buttons on his short trousers at the same time. He scrambled back onto the platform.

'Where?' he yelled. 'Where?'

'Oh,' said Anton mockingly. 'My mistake. It's only a stick. Sorry.'

'You ratbag,' said Christopher.

They began pushing each other again in a friendly joust.

'Boys,' said Pat. 'This is not the time—'

A loud blast from the train's horn drowned her voice.

The small steam engine shunted its way to

the other end of the single carriage. It contacted the boxcar with a clang. The train was preparing to leave. No one spoke. Soon they would be alone.

At that moment a tiny dog trotted up the steps and looked up at them sadly.

The locomotive let out a burst of steam. The dog, startled, ran quickly to the edge of the platform and disappeared under the boxcar.

'Did you see that?' yelled Christopher.

He bent over and peered into the gap between the platform and the train but could see nothing but black stones.

'The train is going,' said Anton.

'We have to get it out,' shouted Christopher.

The conductor disappeared into the train and the noise from the steam engine grew shrill. Christopher began to run towards the back of the carriage.

'Come back,' yelled Pat. 'Come back. You can't risk your life for a dog.'

Christopher ignored her.

He screamed at the invisible driver, 'Don't go, don't go.' But even as the words left his mouth, he knew that there was no way he would be heard over the sound of the panting engine.

Steam hissed between the front wheels. The desperate boy paused and then jumped onto the tracks behind the carriage.

'No,' yelled Pat.

She was too late. Christopher was already squatting down and peering along the dark tunnel between the wheels. At the far end, underneath the boxcar, he could just make out the little dog framed against a small rectangle of light.

He began sprinting along the side of the train. The empty windows flashed by above his head. There was no one to help.

'Don't go, don't go,' he yelled again.

The locomotive's horn shrieked back angrily.

Panting, Christopher threw himself onto the ground next to the boxcar. It was dark under there. He blinked and then saw the dog curled up between the wheels. He couldn't believe it. It was sleeping.

'Here, boy,' he said.

The dog opened one lazy eye but didn't move. Christopher patted his knee.

'Here, boy, here, boy,' he said again.

The dog looked at him in a relaxed way.

'Come on, come on, fellah,' he said urgently.

Still the dog did not move. Christopher shouted every word he could think of.

'Run.'

'Quick.'

'Walk.'

'Heel.'

Still the dog lay curled up.

A whistle sounded. The wheels began to tremble.

Christopher was desperate. He only had seconds. Even less. He couldn't crawl under there. Could he? Was there time? He remembered the bombing during the war and the broken buildings and bodies. No, he couldn't do it.

But there was a chance. Quick, quick, quick.

Yes, throw something. He looked around for a stick but there was nothing nearby.

Think. Think. Think. Oh, yes. He hastily reached into his pocket and pulled out the piece of greasy sausage.

The wheels of the train began to turn.

Christopher broke some off and waved it in front of the dog.

'Yum, yum,' he said. He pitched the sausage towards the forest. The dog shot out from the train and ran after it.

The hungry animal gulped the sausage down and then ran back, looking up for more.

'Sorry boy, that's all for now,' said Christopher. He grabbed the dog by the collar.

'Gotcha,' he said.

He picked up the dog and waited as the train passed and disappeared along the tracks. He climbed back onto the platform and saw a sack labelled MAIL hanging from a nail on a post.

'This is for your own good,' he said. 'We can't have you running off again.' The dog began to lick his face.

Christopher chuckled and put the dog inside the sack. He reached into his pocket, hesitated and then tossed in the last of the sausage.

'You're all alone,' he said to the shape in the sack. 'Abandoned. Like us.'

His mother smiled sadly.

'Don't be such a misery guts,' she said. 'This is the land where dreams come true. We are out of the migrant camp. Anything could happen.'

'That's what I'm worried about,' said Christopher.

The last sounds of the train faded away. All was still. Christopher peered around. The gloomy trees offered nothing but an uncaring silence.

The three of them sat down on their suitcases

and waited. And waited. They brushed away the flies that crawled around their eyes. Sweat ran down their faces.

Anton stared at the dirt road that led into the forest.

'We could start walking,' he said.

His new mother shook her head. 'Too dangerous,' she said.

The dog began to whimper inside the sack.

'He's thirsty,' said Christopher.

'So am I,' said Anton.

They looked at each other helplessly as their situation dawned on them. No water. No food. And no shelter. They were all aware of the stack of supplies that had been left at the end of the platform, but none of them suggested what was on their minds.

Time passed. An hour. And then another. Christopher lifted the dog from the sack and cradled it in his arms.

'Don't worry,' he said. 'Help will come. Then

we will be at the hotel. I can just see it in my mind.'

He closed his eyes.

'It's built out of stone. Cool inside. Leadlight windows, a bellboy in a red uniform to take our cases. A dining room with white tablecloths and waitresses with lacy caps. Roast beef for dinner.'

'With gravy,' said Anton. 'And mashed potato with butter.'

Christopher nodded enthusiastically. 'All followed by apple pie with ice cream and custard. And chilled lemonade.'

'Don't forget the soft beds and crisp sheets,' said Anton.

'You've both been spending too much time dreaming,' laughed their mother. 'It might not be quite as posh as that.'

The visions vanished. They licked their dry lips and stared at the crumbling excuse for a railway station. Christopher put the dog back in the sack.

Anton looked around. 'Where is he?' he said.

No one answered.

'Jeez,' said Christopher. 'This place is creepy. 'Maybe we've made a mistake. Maybe we should go back home.'

'Twelve thousand miles?' said Anton.

'Give it a chance,' said Pat. 'We can make a home here if we try.'

The light began to fade in the sky. Strange squawks erupted from the forest. And then there was another sound.

They all fell silent and listened.

'A motor,' yelled Anton.

The sound grew louder.

'He's here,' said Pat. 'Thank goodness.'

Two

A mud-spattered, rusting truck lumbered
out of the trees. It had a cabin with four doors
and a canvas-covered tray on the back. It pulled
to a stop and a middle-aged man stepped out. He
was wearing grubby shorts, a sweaty blue singlet
and a wide-brimmed, battered hat. He stepped
onto the platform and surveyed the travellers.

'G'day,' he said.

'Good afternoon,' said Pat.

The man looked along the railway track.

'Anyone else get off?' he said.

She shook her head.

'I was expecting someone. I'm picking him up.'

'We're expecting someone too,' she said. She opened her handbag and pulled out a folded piece of paper. She handed it to the man and said, 'Do you know where this is?'

He took the piece of paper. His eyes widened as he read.

THE LAST COACH
Hotel and General Store
HELP WANTED

Applicants must be good with customers.
Able to fillet fish, pull a beer and take a joke.

FREE BOARD AND LODGINGS AND £50 PW.

Apply in writing to PO Box 7
Booly Bool West

He stared at her, not able to take it in.

'You?' he said. 'You're Pat? You're the new bloke?'

'Patricia,' she said firmly.

'No, no, no,' he said. 'Patrick. It's a man's job.' He glanced at the boys. 'And I don't want any…'

He stopped speaking but Christopher finished the sentence for him.

'Kids?' he said.

Pat's face fell. 'We've come all this way. You offered me the job.'

'I'm sorry, love, but you didn't say you were a woman. It's not the place for a… well-spoken lady like you. You'll have to get the next train back.'

They stared straight into each other's eyes. She spoke in a low voice, trying to control herself.

'We came twelve thousand miles to get to this country. And another fifteen hundred to get here by bus and rail. You made a mistake. You advertised for a person to fill a job. I am a person. You didn't say it had to be a man. You owe us. Are you just going to abandon us here?'

He shook his head in confusion.

'When is the next train?' she asked.

He looked at his boots.

'Mundy,' he said slowly.

'Today is Monday.'

He nodded. 'Next Mundy. It only runs once a week.'

'And where are we going to sleep for seven days?' she said. She pointed down at the ground beneath the platform. 'Under here? With the snakes?'

The man looked confused.

'Eastern browns,' he said. 'Deadly poisonous. You wouldn't kip under there.'

She raised a scornful eyebrow. 'I don't scare that easily.'

'Sorry,' he said. 'That was a stupid thing to say. Give me time to think.'

Christopher was aware of his mother's distressed face. His heart went out to her. She had suffered so much. He bent down and picked up his suitcase. Then he jumped onto the track.

'Where are you going, mate?' said the man.

'Back to the migrant hostel,' he said. 'And then home.' He began to walk along the railway track.

'There's tigers too,' said the man.

'Tigers?' yelped Anton.

'Tiger snakes. Deadly,' the man growled. 'And copperheads. One bite and you're gone. And crocs. And mosquitoes. And…' His voice trailed away.

Anton picked up his case. And then his mother's. He put them on the side of the platform and jumped onto the rails with his brother.

He looked at the man.

'We don't care about snakes,' he said. 'We've faced worse. We survived the bombing. And the war. We can handle this. If you've got a bad deal, get out of it. Come on, Pat. We'll walk.'

'Don't,' said the man. He gestured at the rutted road. 'You're right. I owe you one. You can all stay at The Last Coach until the next train.'

'That's very kind of you,' said Pat.

'Mum,' said Christopher under his breath. 'We can't. He doesn't really want us. And it's a whole week.'

The man heard.

Pat ignored Christopher and held out her hand to the man. He took it, perhaps a little shyly, and shook with a soft grasp.

'You already know my name,' she said. 'What's yours?'

'Crayfish,' he said.

She laughed. And he did too. Maybe he was relieved that he had shed some of his guilt.

'Crayfish?' she said. 'What sort of name is that?'

'It's a nickname,' he said cheerfully. 'You only give nicknames to people you like. It's a compliment.'

Christopher scowled and scratched his hairless head. He had memories of unkind nicknames being applied to him. Baldy was one among many.

At that moment there was a squeal from the sack.

'Lonely,' cried the man. 'There you are.'

He ran over to the mailbag and took out the dog, who began to lick his face. He smiled and scratched the dog behind the ears.

'You little devil,' he said. He turned to the three travellers.

'I stopped on the way here to take a ... take a break. And little Lonely disappeared into the bush. That's why I was late. I've been searching everywhere for him. I thought I'd lost him. He's everything to me.'

'Well, you can thank Christopher for that,' said Pat. 'The dog ran under the train. He rescued Lonely just in time.'

'Yes,' said Anton. 'He threw a sausage into the bush and the dog went after it.'

The man grinned. 'Food is the only thing that will move him. He'll chase a sausage. Or a bone. But he won't do anything else you say. He drives you crazy with it.'

Crayfish patted Christopher on the shoulder. 'Thanks a million,' he said. 'I really love this little fellah.'

His voice was shaking.

'You can help out in the pub until the next train,' he said to Pat. 'But don't get your hopes up. It's no place for a sensitive woman like you.'

'You don't know what I'm capable of,' she said quietly.

He didn't seem to know what to say. He turned to Christopher.

'You should be wearing a hat,' he said. 'With that bald head you won't last a day in the tropical sun.'

Christopher flushed.

'It's called hypotrichosis,' he said indignantly.

'I haven't heard of that, son,' Crayfish said softly. 'But take a look at this.'

He pulled off his hat and revealed his own hairless head. He grinned but Christopher didn't return it. Being bald when you are a man is not the same. He had only just met this person but could sense his feelings changing like a thermometer. At the moment the temperature was definitely cool.

'Come on,' said Crayfish. 'Let's go. I was only expecting one…er, passenger. But there's room in the truck for three.'

A muffled yelp came from Lonely.

'Four,' he said. 'Make that four.'

He released a metal canteen that was attached to his belt and poured water into his hat. The dog lapped furiously.

'Good fellah,' said Crayfish. He put the wet hat back on his head and handed the water bottle around. They all gulped thirstily.

Crayfish walked towards the pile of boxes and sacks. 'Come on, men,' he said. 'You can earn your keep. Give me a hand.'

Both boys began loading the boxes of supplies onto the truck. 'Leave the anchor,' said Crayfish. 'There's not enough room. I'll get it next Mundy when I bring you back.'

Pat started to carry a sack of flour over to the truck.

'Not you,' Crayfish said.

She gave him a stare and then said, 'I worked with soldiers in the war. I'm as good as any man.'

He nodded. 'Fair enough,' he said. Then he added, 'Pat.'

She smiled. Christopher scowled. Why did his mother waste a smile on this rough character? He suddenly thought of his father – smart, brave and polite. And dead. He blinked back a tear. And this place. He knew he could never call it home.

When they had finished loading the truck, Crayfish climbed in behind the wheel and turned on the headlights. Darkness had fallen suddenly. As if someone had thrown a switch.

'Jump in,' he said. 'It's a long way. We'll have to sleep out in the bush for the night.'

The two boys climbed into the back seat, leaving Pat to sit next to Crayfish. The dog immediately curled up on the floor at their feet.

The engine burst into life and they lurched onto the track. The headlights lit up a narrow corridor between the trees. The forest was dark and sombre.

'So, what's your story, Pat?' said Crayfish.

'What brings gentlefolk like you to this wild country?' His tone was friendly.

'Our story?' said Christopher in a low tone. 'Our story. I'll tell you our story. Our home town is a bombed ruin. My wonderful father is dead. So is my twin brother. Anton's whole family is dead. He ran off from a cruel boys' home. We met him on a ship and he fell overboard. Then we adopted him.'

Crayfish's eyes widened. 'Jeez,' he muttered. 'What happened?'

'He saved me,' said Anton. 'And—'

Christopher cut across Anton, almost shouting. 'When we got to this country we were sent to a migrant hostel in the middle of nowhere. The three of us lived in one tiny room. It was boiling hot in the summer. Freezing in the winter. No shops, no transport, not even a blade of grass. And no way out.'

'Unless I found a job,' said Pat quietly. 'And I did. I answered the ad you put in the paper.

Your offer of work at The Last Coach was enough to get us released.'

She turned around and shook her head at Christopher, trying to cool his outburst. But it didn't work. There was no stopping him.

'And now you want to send us back to the migrant hostel,' he went on. 'I don't want to go back there. I want to go home.'

'We can't go home,' said Pat. 'You know we can't.'

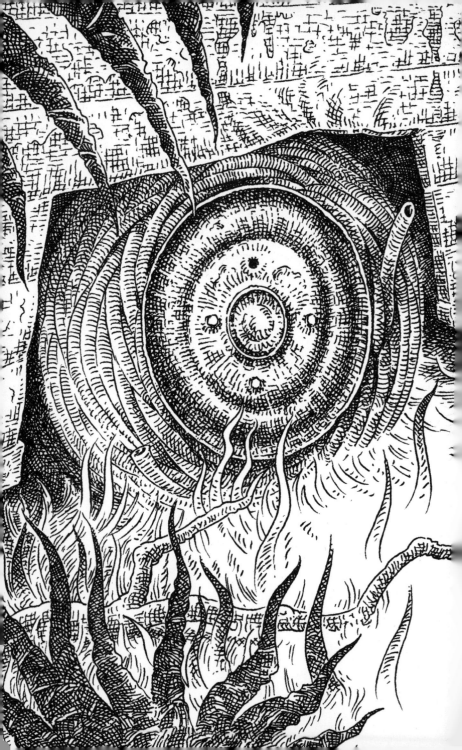

Three

They all sat in silence as the truck began to climb into the mountains. Crayfish changed gear and the engine growled.

'I need to pee,' said Christopher.

The truck came to a halt. Christopher opened the door and stepped into the night.

The forest was black and silent. He walked to the back of the truck where no one could see him and began to undo his trouser buttons. A loud thump made him gasp. An unknown wild creature bounded past.

Christopher gave a scream and scrambled back into the truck.

Crayfish scoffed.

'It's just a roo,' he said. 'They're harmless.'

He drove on, looking for another place to stop.

'Here we are,' he said. 'Have another go.'

Once again Christopher stepped out into the darkness.

Three faces stared out of the cab.

'Don't look,' he said.

A sudden thunder of hooves filled the air as five or six huge shapes galloped past. Christopher screamed again and rushed back to the truck.

Crayfish chuckled softly. Pat gave him a friendly dig in the ribs. 'Don't,' she said softly. 'He's embarrassed.'

'Wild brumbies,' said Crayfish. He began to laugh. He couldn't help himself.

'It's not funny,' said Christopher.

'Sorry,' said Crayfish. 'Look, reach under the seat. There's an empty beer bottle there somewhere. You can do it in that.'

'You're joking,' said Christopher.

Despite his words, he found the bottle. He could feel his face burning with shame as he emptied himself into it. Anton grinned but said nothing.

The truck ploughed on, higher and higher, crawling through the night. Finally, Crayfish turned off into a small clearing and killed the engine.

A decaying caravan was revealed by the headlights. It had no tyres. Instead, long lengths of thick garden hose had been wrapped around the wheels. The caravan had cracked windows that were covered in cobwebs.

'Our overnight accommodation,' Crayfish said. 'The locals stay here in emergencies. But it's used mainly by me and sometimes passing ferals.'

'Ferals?' said Anton.

'Pig hunters. Rough as guts. But don't worry. We'll be okay here for the night. There's bunks and some blankets. You lot can sleep inside. Me and Lonely will kip in the truck.'

He stepped out and returned holding a kerosene lantern, which glowed softly with a yellow light. He handed it to Christopher. 'Here you go,' he said. 'The caravan's not locked.'

Christopher held out the half-filled beer bottle. 'Would you like a drink?' he said.

Crayfish gave him a penetrating look and began to raise the beer bottle to his lips.

'No,' yelled Christopher. He struck the bottle and it fell to the ground with a soft thump.

There was a moment of silence, then Crayfish grinned. 'I only drink Four-Ex,' he said.

'You fell for it,' said Christopher. 'You were going to drink my p—'

'No way,' said Crayfish. 'There's no flies on me, mate.'

'But you can see where they've been,' said Christopher.

They both started to laugh.

Pat was laughing too. Crayfish looked at her approvingly.

'I like a sheila with a sense of humour,' he said.

'Sheila?' she growled.

He grinned sheepishly. 'Okay, woman.'

Christopher headed for the caravan, pulled open the door and looked inside. He fell backwards with a scream and landed on his back. Then he turned over onto his hands and knees and began to vomit.

'What is it?' yelled Anton. 'What, what, what?'

Christopher was dry retching and couldn't get his breath. Finally, he gasped, 'Something dead. With its guts hanging out. And flies everywhere.'

Suddenly a loud blast filled the air.

'A shotgun,' said Pat.

'The ruddy ferals,' said Crayfish. 'Shooting wild pigs. Nothin' to worry about.'

He rushed over to the caravan and came out with one hand held over his mouth and nose.

'It's a whopping big boar. There's maggots everywhere,' he yelped. 'It's been there for ages.' He looked around the campsite.

'The ferals have moved on. They're squatting somewhere else.'

Another two blasts echoed through the dark trees.

'Double barrelled,' said Pat.

Crayfish looked at her, puzzled.

'You lot get into the truck,' he said. 'I'll get rid of the boar.'

The two boys scrambled into the truck and shut the doors. Crayfish tied a large handkerchief across his nose, took a deep breath and started towards the caravan.

Pat tied a thin scarf around her face. She followed Crayfish and tapped him on the shoulder. He turned and raised an eyebrow. Then he nodded, hesitated and led the way into the caravan.

The boys stared out with horrified expressions. The caravan, illuminated in the yellow glow of the headlights, rocked slightly on its hose-covered wheels. There was a sound of scraping and grunting. Pat emerged, stepping down backwards from the door. She moved gingerly, holding on tightly to the back legs of the pig, which was shedding entrails and showers of maggots. Crayfish followed, holding the front legs. The boar's eyeless head lolled to one side and its curled tusks scraped the ground.

Christopher closed his eyes but the terrible

sight remained with him. This new land was supposed to offer a haven of peace and promise. Not an untamed wilderness of snakes, maggots and fear.

Pat and Crayfish staggered into the darkness with the boar. After a short while they emerged, puffing but saying nothing. They climbed into the truck and Crayfish started the engine. The truck lurched forward, made a wide arc and continued along the track, leaving the caravan behind with its door still hanging open.

'I'll never get the stink out,' said Crayfish. 'That caravan's finished.'

'I could get it out,' said Pat. 'I've dealt with much worse than a dead pig.'

It started to rain. Heavily. There was no wind and it was still warm and clammy. The windscreen wipers scraped from side to side, not properly clearing the flooding water from the glass.

They drove in silence through the dark forest. Crayfish looked over his shoulder at the boys and saw that they were already slumped on the seat with closed eyes. He lowered his voice.

'You've got guts, I'll give you that. But this is a hard land. It's beautiful but dangerous. And there's not much company. It can get lonely.'

'Have you family?' said Pat.

He leaned towards the windscreen and seemed to be peering out as if he had seen something on the dark track. Finally, he spoke.

'I did have. Peggy,' he said.

'Peggy?' she queried.

'Me wife. You know. The Bot called her Peg but her real name was Peggy.'

'The Bot?'

'Yeah, The Bot,' he said. 'He smokes OP's.'

'OP's?'

'Other people's. He bots cigarettes.'

She laughed out loud. He ignored her and went on with the story.

'There's three of us run the pub. There's me, The Bot – he's me best mate – and then there's The Beard.'

'What about Peggy?'

'She drowned seven years ago,' he said slowly. 'This place killed her. We searched everywhere but her body was never found.'

In the back seat Christopher opened his eyes. And listened.

'I'm so sorry,' Pat said quietly.

'What about you?' he asked.

'My husband was killed on D-Day,' she said.

'That's tough,' he said. 'Really tough.'

Four

When dawn broke a wonderful sight greeted the weary travellers. A golden sun was rising from the sea beneath a towering sky. The track before them curled along the side of a mountain like a dusty snake clinging to a precipice. The cliff on the left-hand side was sheer and dropped onto a white beach. The boys gazed out of the truck window nervously.

'It is beautiful,' said Pat. 'You're right about that.'

'And hot,' said Christopher.

'Not like home,' said Anton cheerfully. 'Not a snowflake in sight.'

Crayfish put the truck into gear and began the descent of the winding, narrow track.

After four hours of slow driving the track reached sea level, and for a while ran along a muddy mangrove shore. Finally, around noon, they stopped outside a large shed made of corrugated iron. It had two heavy iron doors but no windows. A sign hung over the top.

THE LAST COACH
Hotel and General Store

'What's it say?' said Anton.

Christopher, who had been teaching his brother to read, shook his head in disbelief.

'It's where we are staying,' he said. 'The Last Coach.'

'Last Hope, more like it,' said Anton.

Crayfish stepped out of the car followed by the others. Lonely trotted after him, sniffing the ground as he went.

'Get a load of this,' said Crayfish. He pulled open the doors and waved at the interior enthusiastically.

They stared in astonishment, not knowing what to say.

'What is it?' said Anton.

'Home,' said Crayfish.

The three travellers looked around in silence.

The large tin shed had a dirt floor. The left wall was covered by rough shelves holding glasses and a variety of bottles. These protected by a long wooden bar. Bare log tables were scattered across the eating area. At the back was a battered piano.

On the opposite side of the shed was the

general store. Here, a long counter separated customers from packets and tins of foodstuffs stacked up the wall in open boxes.

A flock of coloured parrots flew inside and began noisily pecking at the litter in the dirt. Lonely ran among them as if they were old friends. They largely ignored him.

'He should be called Friendly,' said Anton.

'A good word,' said Pat. 'Friendly.'

Crayfish grinned. 'Like you,' he said.

Christopher scowled.

In the centre of the room was an enormous welded-steel barbecue attached to a gas bottle.

Christopher surveyed the pub and shook his head.

'We can't sleep here,' he said.

'You're right about that,' said Crayfish. 'Follow me.'

As they left the pub, Crayfish indicated another dilapidated shed with half its roof missing.

'That's the long-drop,' he said.

'Long-drop?' said Christopher. 'What's that?'

'Er, toilets. And a shower. We share with the customers.'

They began to walk along a dirt path that ran through brightly coloured vines and drooping eucalypts. Finally, they reached a crumbling asbestos-lined bungalow with a long verandah looking out to sea.

'There's two empty rooms,' he said. 'I set the first one up for the new man – er, worker. That's Pat's. The other one is a spare for rough nuts who drink too much and can't make it home. The boys can have that. Get your things, unpack and have a rest. I'll bring you some grub.'

The boys made their way to their room. It was not quite what Christopher had imagined. To say the least. There were two rickety camp stretchers covered with smelly army blankets. An open window had only a bamboo blind to keep out the buzzing insects. The air was humid. In the corner was a clutch of brooms, buckets and mops.

After they had settled, Crayfish arrived with some cheese, ham and pineapple slices, which they quickly gobbled. In no time the boys were asleep, exhausted from the journey.

*   *   *

When they awoke it was dark. The sound of the generator hummed through the trees and voices in the bar floated above it like the blurred words of a distant choir. Pat knocked on the door of their room.

'Come on,' she said. 'Get dressed, I'm hungry.'

They made their way back to the pub with her. The front doors were wide open to let in the night sky and a fresh breeze off the sea.

The boys were in their best clothes: neatly creased shorts, short-sleeved shirts and shiny black shoes. Pat wore a classy coloured scarf around her head that she had bought when the boat stopped in Ceylon.

'We should have come casual,' she said with an ironic smile as she surveyed the men at the bar – some with bare feet and all wearing blue singlets and shorts. She walked behind the long counter and grabbed the handle of the single beer tap. The men looked at her expectantly.

'Who's for a pint?' she said.

A laugh went up.

'I think you mean a schooner,' said a whiskery man. 'And make it cold.'

Pat tipped up a glass and filled it with a flourish.

Crayfish introduced her. 'This is Pat and her two boys. They'll be helping out for a few days.'

'Where's the new bloke?' said the whiskery man.

'That'll be me,' said Pat with a grin.

Crayfish gave a foolish chuckle and whacked a hand down on the bemused man's shoulder.

'This is The Beard. The young bloke over there by the barbie is The Bot.'

Crayfish handed Anton a pair of tongs and

a huge fork. 'Here,' he said. 'You two look after the snags.'

'Snags?' said Christopher.

'Mystery bags,' said Pat cheerfully.

'You're picking up the lingo,' said Crayfish approvingly.

'Ah, sausages,' said Anton.

Crayfish put a hand on each boy's shoulder and gave them a gentle push towards the barbecue.

'Off you go,' he said.

He smiled at Pat.

'You don't have to work tonight,' he said. 'Just join in and get to know people.'

The boys stared hungrily at the sizzling sausages. Anton enjoyed turning them over and putting them onto a slice of bread for the customers. They were a rough but cheery mob.

The Bot gave a toss of his tangled hair. He had a snake tattooed on his chest and neck. The head of the snake covered his voice box and when he spoke it seemed to open and shut its mouth.

'Eat up while you can, boys,' he said. 'The place is closed tomorrow.'

'Why is that?' said Anton.

'It's Wednesday,' he answered. 'Crayfish always goes off in the truck on Wednesday.'

At that moment a loud chord rang out from the piano. Christopher looked up.

It was Pat. She started playing an old tune – 'Show Me the Way to Go Home'.

A cheer went up and in no time a crowd had surrounded her and was singing loudly. Lonely began to howl an accompaniment.

'I didn't know Pat could play the piano,' said Anton.

'She talks posh,' said Christopher. 'But Mum has mixed with all sorts. She drove an ambulance in the war and tried to cheer up wounded soldiers.'

As the evening progressed, Anton and Christopher began to tire.

'Off to bed,' said Pat. 'I'll see you in the morning.'

Back in their room the boys lay looking up at the ceiling, from which one small light globe hung. The window was open and the moist air made everything they touched feel damp. Mosquitoes buzzed in the gloom.

'You should give him a break,' said Anton.

'Who?'

'You know who. Crayfish.'

'What have I done?' said Christopher.

'You don't laugh at his jokes. You frown when Pat does laugh at them. When you gave out the snags you handed him the two burnt ones. He's not a bad bloke.'

With that, Anton turned over and was soon asleep, but Christopher lay staring at the dim globe with unfocused eyes.

Something moved.

A beautiful black moth with enormous wings had settled on the ceiling. A small lizard also clung there, hanging on with delicate toes. It was stationary, watching, not betraying its presence. Every now and then it would move just one leg, slowly drawing closer to the moth.

Christopher had never seen a lizard that could walk upside down. He couldn't take his eyes off it. He was just about to jump up and save the moth, but he was too late.

The lizard had shot out an enormously long tongue and pulled the moth into its mouth. There was a tiny fluttering of black wings and then it was gone.

'Aagh,' he screamed.

In the nearby bed Anton groaned but did not wake.

Christopher's head spun.

The world was a bleak place. Death and deception could strike at any time.

There was something wrong with Crayfish's story about his dead wife and he couldn't quite figure it out. But there was one thing he knew for sure.

Crayfish was not going to get the moth. His mother was not there for the taking.

Five

The next morning Christopher awoke to find himself alone. Anton had disappeared. Christopher guessed that he was already at the pub, stuffing down cold sausages.

He quickly dressed and walked towards the store. He was surprised to see a number of scruffy men heading towards the long-drop. They looked as if they had been sleeping rough, either in the bush somewhere or in the wounded cars that were scattered under the trees.

The boy was busting to sit down and relieve himself, so he followed them into the battered building. His jaw dropped in surprise and confusion. He could feel a red flush creeping up his neck.

The toilets were made up of one long, wide plank in which six holes had been cut. The first four were occupied by men already sitting there with their pants around their feet. The Bot was one of them.

He looked up and grinned. 'Help yourself, mate,' he said in a friendly, rasping voice. The tattoo of the snake on his neck opened and closed its mouth.

The man next to him lowered the paper he

was reading and added his own welcome. He farted loudly.

A red-headed youth sitting nearby sensed Christopher's discomfort. He felt moved to give the newcomer a piece of advice.

'Don't fall in. It's a long way down and no one's going to reach in and pull you out by the hair.' They all began to chuckle.

Christopher's face burned. It was not the first time he had heard a joke about his lack of hair.

The Bot scowled at the youth and then spoke to the other man.

'Hey, Dave,' he said. 'You haven't got a spare smoke, have ya?'

Dave lowered his newspaper, sighed and handed over a packet of cigarettes.

Christopher was confused and embarrassed. Never in his life had he been faced with sitting on a toilet that had no door. Even during the worst of the war back home he had been able to creep off to a private space behind a tree or a fence.

He had experienced terror in the Blitz when the bombers came over. But that seemed nothing beside the prospect of pulling down his pants and sitting next to these crude men. Dave suddenly let out a satisfied, 'Ah.'

A soft plop came from the pit far below.

'That's better,' he said.

The distressed boy could not join them. He turned and rushed out, followed by laughter. 'You'll be back,' shouted Dave. 'Sooner or later you'll be back.'

Christopher let his belt out a notch and made his way to the store.

His mother, Anton and Crayfish were just finishing off an egg and bacon breakfast. The three of them were laughing.

'G'day,' said Crayfish. 'Come and get some grub. Make yourself at home. See you later, Pat,' he said. 'You've made a good start.'

They exchanged a warm glance. He shoved the wide-brimmed hat onto his bald head and walked towards the truck.

'See you later,' Pat called out happily.

Christopher frowned and dropped into a seat.

'Have you seen the toilets here?' He shook his head in disbelief. 'They're incredible.'

'A good place to make new friends,' said Anton.

Christopher's eyes opened wide. 'You went?'

Anton nodded. 'When in Rome...'

'Don't worry about it,' said Pat. 'Use the ladies'.'

'What?' said Christopher. 'Never.'

She gave him a kindly smile. 'You might have noticed that there's not many women around here. You'll be okay.'

Christopher blushed.

'But there will be one day,' she said. 'This place has potential. Look at the reefs. Look at the beaches. Look at the clear blue sky and the trees. In the winter it's warm and lovely. It's a paradise.'

He stared out. It was true.

The forest surrounding them dropped onto a golden beach. A brilliant blue and green sea was dotted with coral reefs and densely wooded islands. Brightly coloured butterflies flitted crookedly through the air while birds of every hue tried to match their splendour. Only twenty yards away a sea turtle was slowly scraping a hole in the sand with its back flipper.

'It might be nice now,' said Christopher, 'but up here things can change just like ...'

He snapped his fingers.

In an instant the sun vanished and rain began to fall.

'That,' said Christopher with an amazed grin. He stood up and bowed, pleased that nature had provided him with a joke.

They all laughed.

'Do it again,' said Anton.

Christopher shook his head with a smile.

They wouldn't have heard him even if had spoken. The sky had opened up. The sea and the distant islands were obscured by the downpour. The rain fell so heavily that the small pub seemed to be the only thing that existed in the universe. It thundered on the tin roof.

Paradise was nowhere to be seen.

* * *

A week passed. Nothing had changed. And everything had changed.

No one mentioned the fact that they had not been packed off on the next train. So, Pat had the job for at least another seven days.

Christopher stared out from the pub. They were all sitting around the table eating a meal that Crayfish had prepared – cold roast pork with apple sauce, potatoes and canned vegetables.

The constant rain had not stopped once in a week. And the damp heat continued all day and night. Mosquitoes made it impossible to sleep, as did the noise of the coarse men and a few women drinking and singing until midnight.

These people travelled great distances to reach the only pub for a hundred miles. There were fishermen from the cray boats that pulled in for supplies and workers from a far-off lumber mill.

A group of Aboriginal people had a camp nearby. And scattered through the forest were a few families living in caravans and tents. These campers scratched a living from the forest and shot feral pigs, which they sold to Crayfish.

Basically, the pub was a small island in a huge ocean of trees.

Pat was getting on well with Crayfish. They joked and teased each other a lot and she even played the old piano while he sang to the customers in the evenings. He had a deep, strong voice that could be heard above the noisy group, who often clapped and cheered his renditions.

Crayfish, The Beard and The Bot had started making changes to the pub. They had taken down the huge front doors and framed up a wall where these had once been. There were spaces for windows and a regular door.

'Next comes a new toilet,' said Pat, throwing a look at Christopher.

'And then a wooden floor,' said Crayfish.

'What about a library?' said Anton, who was reading the only book in the place for the second time. 'I'm getting a bit sick of *The World's Best Pubs*.'

'Library,' scoffed Crayfish. 'Hardly anyone around here can read.'

'I can,' said Anton proudly. 'Well, just about.'

Christopher didn't join in the conversation. He knew he was sulking but he couldn't help it. There was something about Crayfish that wasn't right. No one ever mentioned Peggy. Maybe it was because Crayfish missed his dead wife so much and they were just respecting the grieving man's feelings. Or was there some other reason they never spoke about her?

A row of battered trucks was parked outside and the occupants, all men from the timber mill, were making the best of the bar.

Christopher's stomach still had the hard pain that began in the toilet block a week ago.

He had not been able to go into the long-drop toilet and sit there next to The Beard or The Bot or any other customer who might wander in. He had been down there and got as far as dropping his pants. But every time he had heard approaching voices he pulled them up and hurried out.

He had tried to relieve himself behind a tree, but the unending rain was heavy and Pat scolded him for getting wet. After two days he had constipation and by now he was really in trouble. He needed to get onto a toilet seat and sit there until the deed was done.

The pain in his guts was becoming unbearable. He glanced outside and saw that the rain had stopped.

There was not one woman in the place except for his mother. He looked across at the toilet block. He jumped up and made a dash towards the ladies' loo, followed by Lonely. He disappeared inside and shut the door after the dog.

The Ladies' had no cubicles, just one proper toilet with a shiny brown seat. He lowered his pants and sat. He patted Lonely, who started to lick his hand.

'You are the only one in this place who knows how I feel,' he said to the dog.

As if wanting to cheer the boy up, Lonely jumped onto Christopher's lap.

'I've never sat on a toilet with a dog before,' said Christopher.

Voices floated over the partition from the men's side. He recognised them at once.

'Have you got a spare smoke?' said The Bot.

There was a sigh from The Beard and then the sound of a match striking.

'What do you think about the new woman?' said The Bot.

'A bit of all right,' said The Beard. 'A really great sheila.'

'Her lads are okay too. Nice boys.'

'The bald one's a bit shy. But he'll fit in once he gets used to the place.'

'Tomorrow is Wednesday,' said The Bot. 'So, Crayfish will be off at the crack of dawn as usual.'

'To visit Peggy?'

'Yes.'

'She's looking terrific.'

'He's a lucky bloke. She's a beauty.'

'With a great bottom.'

'I wish she was mine.'

'No hope of that, mate. Not in a million years.'

They both chuckled.

'Well,' said The Bot, 'we can't sit here all day. The rain's stopped so let's get that wall down.'

Christopher was still sitting on the ladies' toilet with the dog on his lap. His head began to swim. The men he had overheard seemed friendly. But really, they were insensitive brutes. Describing people by their physical characteristics. He knew his mother would be outraged.

But worst of all, Crayfish's wife was not dead. And he was flirting with Christopher's mother. Crayfish was a liar.

Well, if Crayfish was going to visit his wife in the morning, Christopher would follow him. But first he would have to get his bowels moving. He tightened his stomach muscles and pushed.

'Ah,' he said. 'That's better.' He heard the sound of a plop far below and shuddered.

A dark thought entered his head. He was in danger of turning into one of these men himself. These long-drop toilets were terrible. And so were the men. He had to get away from this place.

At that moment there was another, louder sound. Someone was banging furiously on the outside wall. He heard a familiar voice.

'Knock out the props,' yelled The Beard.

There was another loud bang and the wall in front of Christopher began to move. It swung outwards and fell flat on the ground with an enormous crash.

Looking straight at him were the two amazed men and a small crowd from the timber mill who were just leaving the pub after lunch. A startled cry went up at the sight of Christopher sitting there in the open with his pants down and a dog on his lap.

A roar of laughter filled the air.

Christopher, red in the face, jumped to his feet and desperately pulled up his pants. Lonely leapt at him playfully.

The onlookers' cackling grew even louder. The Beard had fallen on the ground, holding his sides with mirth.

This was the most embarrassing thing that had ever happened to Christopher. There had to be something he could do to beat the shrieks of merriment. His mind spun. He wanted to run into the forest and hide his shame. But his survival instinct kicked in. Years of teasing about his bald head had taught him to use every weapon he had. And there was only one available.

Humour.

He bent over, picked up Lonely and held him under one arm. Then he did a little tap dance and bowed to his audience.

The applause was loud and genuine. Now the crowd was laughing with him, not at him.

But inside, Christopher was not amused.

He hated this crude place of secrets and lies. And he wanted to know the truth about Crayfish and his wife, Peggy.

Six

Christopher went back to his room and thought about confronting Crayfish. He needed to be careful. If he caused a big fuss Pat would turn against him for being rude. And he had to get his facts straight.

There were two things for sure. Crayfish was flirting with his mother. And he already had a wife whom he visited every Wednesday.

He had to say something. He couldn't help himself. He ran down to the long-drop toilet where Crayfish was banging nails into the new wall.

'I know about Peggy,' he blurted out.

Crayfish looked at him. 'So?' he said.

'So, stop flirting with my mother,' he shouted. 'Leave her alone. You've already got a wife.'

'You don't know what you're talking about,' said Crayfish. 'Look…'

The boy wasn't listening. He was already running across the grass towards the bungalow.

Christopher avoided Crayfish for the rest of the day. That night he tossed and turned in his bed. Crayfish was guilty as charged. But he had not owned up about Peggy. Christopher had to prove that Crayfish's wife was still alive.

All night the rain drummed on the roof. Finally the dawn broke, dark and grey. He dressed quietly so as not to wake Anton. He quickly scribbled a note and left it on the end of his brother's bed.

He heard a car door slam. It was Crayfish, leaving in the truck. Christopher rushed along the verandah and sprinted through the rain. The truck was shaking gently, with a whiff of smoke rising from the exhaust pipe.

Christopher ran to the passenger's side of the truck and scrambled inside. Lonely was curled up on the floor. He looked up and wagged his tail as the boy slammed the door behind him.

'What are you doing here?' growled Crayfish.

'We didn't finish our conversation,' said Christopher.

'You've said enough already.'

'It's important.'

Crayfish answered slowly, giving weight to every word.

'This is not a good time,' he said. 'I have to get going.'

'Not before you've heard what I have to say.'

'No,' said Crayfish. His voice was urgent. And forceful. 'There's a cyclone off the coast. And we've had heavy rain. Really heavy rain. For a long time. And there's going to be a king tide.'

'So?' said Christopher.

'So, when those three things combine the tide rushes up the river. And meets the flooding water coming downstream. Where they meet the water rises. Quickly. There's a big flood. Last time it happened someone drowned. I have to go and … check on things.'

'I don't believe you,' said Christopher.

Crayfish reached over and opened the passenger door. He put his hand on the boy's shoulder and pushed. Christopher was firmly ejected. He landed on his feet, just managing to stay upright.

There was a crunching of gears and the truck started to move.

Christopher felt white-hot anger flush through his head. He had to know what Crayfish was up to. Where was he going? And where was Peggy? He began to run after the vehicle. He grabbed the tailgate and was dragged along. The toes of his shoes scraped through the mud. The truck slowed momentarily and he was able to pull himself up and scramble in.

The enormity of what he was doing suddenly swept over him. He didn't know where he was going. If he was caught he would be at the mercy of Crayfish's anger. But it was too late. They were on their way.

The back of the truck was bare except for an empty backpack. There was no window between the front cabin and the tray so Crayfish wouldn't be able to catch sight of him in his rear-vision mirror. He was safe. For now.

But it was no use pretending. He had done something stupid.

He was soaking wet but the air was warm.

So unlike what he was used to – rain falling in the winter the way it should, not in the summer like this weird place.

The rain outside was a thick curtain, stopping him from seeing more than a few feet away.

The truck bumped along the narrow track, splashing through puddles and wheel ruts. At times it groaned up winding hills but after about an hour it began to descend. His view was only out of the back of the truck. He longed to see more of where he was. Could he risk it?

There was a sudden break in the rain. Through the trees he could see that they were moving along the side of a valley. They were slightly above a river, which was wide and flowing strongly. He stuck his head out of the back of the truck and looked towards the front. Far in the distance he could see a grey sea beneath a dark sky.

Without warning the truck stopped. The engine died and the boy heard the squeal of a handbrake being applied.

He heard Crayfish speak. 'Come here, Lonely. Come here, boy.'

Christopher had to get out before he was discovered. He jumped to the ground, stumbled and fell. He scrambled into the thick, wet rainforest and lay on his stomach, not daring to breathe.

Finally, he gained the courage to raise himself and peer through the undergrowth. Crayfish was staring at the river. He turned and looked in Christopher's direction. The boy sank down, not daring to move again.

After a few more minutes he heard the engine start. The truck began to move. He jumped to his feet but the truck was already gaining speed. He began to run after it. But it was useless.

'Stop,' he yelled. 'Stop.'

The truck did not stop. In just a few seconds everything had changed. He was alone in the middle of a dense forest. With no food. And no one to help. He began walking along the muddy track in the direction taken by the truck. The track ran alongside the river, which was wide and deep. He walked along carefully, trying to avoid the flooded wheel ruts.

His head began to spin and his legs ached. For a moment the world seemed to take on a dreamlike, impossible reality. He stared at the river. Something was wrong. Something was out of place. Then it clicked.

It was flowing backwards. Away from the sea.

At that moment the rain began to fall again. The drenching, warm rain.

He stumbled on. And on. And on. Several hours passed. His feet were sore inside his sodden shoes. His trousers rubbed his thighs like sheets of sandpaper. He breathed with loud, panting gasps.

Still no sign of the truck. The river was no longer in view but he could hear its strong, gurgling flow off to his left. To his right the forest rose almost vertically: a rocky, green wall of lush plants cut by tumbling, splashing streams.

And then, just as he was about to collapse and give up, the track dipped and widened into a small clearing surrounded by large gum trees. And there was the truck. Parked by the river with its front wheels in the rising water. Surely Crayfish had not left it like that?

A quick glance showed him that Crayfish's backpack was gone. Instead, hanging up on a rope in the back of the truck were about a dozen dresses. Women's clothes.

Now his suspicions were confirmed. There was a woman here. And Crayfish was moving her out.

Seven

Christopher turned his attention back to
the river, trying to make sense of what he was
looking at. Many of the trees were growing out
of the water, which was still slowly surging in
the wrong direction, carrying logs and tangled
root balls upstream.

He suddenly became aware of something on the edge of his vision. It was so out of place that he hesitated to look directly at it.

There was something in one of the trees.

The swollen river lapped high up the trunk. A rough ladder made of planks was nailed to it.

And there, held aloft by the gnarled fingers of its spreading branches, was...a large fishing boat.

A boat stuck in a tree. Christopher's mind reeled. He fought for clarity. Think. Think. Take stock. Don't panic.

The same strength that had once led him to dive off a passenger ship to save Anton now clicked into place. Think. And then act.

The boat was in good shape, considering where it was. The whole of the front half had been freshly painted while the rear section, which was higher off the ground, was peeling and faded. The main damage seemed to be a spot just below the portholes, where a branch had punctured the wooden hull. It resembled an arm punched through a wall by an angry man.

The rain was still falling steadily and the river seemed to be swirling rather than flowing. The water had now reached halfway up the front wheels of the truck, which was clearly in danger of being swallowed. He hesitated. He could try to start the motor but he had never driven a truck before.

'Crayfish,' he yelled. 'Crayfish. Come and move the truck.' He screamed over and over but there was no reply.

Christopher ran to the river and began to wade into the water. It was soon up to his waist, then his armpits as he neared the tree. The powerful current was pulling at his legs. He strode forward and just managed to grab one of the nailed planks. He began scrambling and in no time was in the branches. He crawled along an outstretched branch and dropped onto the deck.

He looked around, now calm. Assessing the situation. Ready for the worst. What if Peggy was really dead? But still here? In this boat?

Images of mummies and dead bodies floated through his mind. He shook the thoughts away and looked around the deck.

Apart from a broken mast and the hole in its side, the fishing boat seemed to be well cared for. Everything was in its place, with coils of rope ready for use. Christopher noticed a few steps leading up to a bridge and two more descending to a closed cabin door.

A wooden hatch cover had been removed from its place over the hold. The opening had a temporary canvas stretched over it.

Stacked by the railing were a number of household items, all drenched by the rain. There was a small stool. A painting of a vase of flowers. A gilded mirror. And a box of women's shoes.

He quickly walked down the two steps to the cabin and stepped inside.

It was deserted. Off to one side was a small door with the word GALLEY written on it.

He looked around for any sign of Crayfish but there was none. The floor sloped slightly, making it feel as if the boat had been caught side-on by a giant wave. He noted every feature: a table bolted to the floor, a map pinned on the wall, a brass compass fixed to a bench and one double bed.

But most obvious was the branch that had punched through the side of the boat. It had been sawn off neatly and the stump filled the hole like a plug.

On a small bench was a picture of a pretty young woman in a wedding dress. She was holding the hand of her new husband, smiling for the camera. The groom had a beard and a full head of black hair. Two decorative candles stood next to the frame.

Christopher picked up the photograph. He was sure that he had seen the man before. With a flash of insight, he realised. It was Crayfish. Younger, but definitely Crayfish.

The cabin had many feminine touches. The kitchen table was covered in a gingham cloth set out for two people with fine plates decorated with flowers. A frilly nightdress was draped over a chair. An open cupboard revealed a half-full rack of pretty dresses.

The whole room reminded him of something but he couldn't quite bring it to mind. It was more like a tiny chapel than a cabin. A shrine, perhaps?

He pushed the thought out of his head and peered through the porthole. It was still raining heavily. The forest was dark, even though the day was not yet half over. Some coloured birds were sheltering from the rain in the nearby branches. The tree swayed and the boat moved gently with it.

Where was Crayfish? He had to tell him that the truck was in danger of being swamped.

He pushed open the galley door and gasped. Crayfish was sitting on a small chair wrapping a torn sheet around his left leg. Blood was already seeping through the cloth. He had clearly broken his leg and was splinting it.

Lonely, who was curled up on the floor, looked up happily as the boy entered.

Crayfish seemed confused. He shook his head in despair. He held up a warning hand and finished tying off the torn sheet. Then he spoke.

'Help me up on deck,' he said. He stood and put one arm around the boy's neck. Together they hobbled through the cabin and out into the rain.

They both stared over the edge of the boat. The water had risen so high that only the top of the truck could be seen. Below them, on the trunk of the tree, just six or seven rungs of the ladder were showing above the surface.

'It's too late,' groaned Crayfish. 'We'll never get to the shore.'

Christopher took a step backwards towards the canvas cover over the hold.

'Don't step on that,' ordered Crayfish, 'or you'll go straight down.'

The boat was now bobbing about, held in the air by the branches as if it were at sea in a swell. The treetops surrounded it like a heaving ocean.

'Take me below,' Crayfish said. 'There's nothing we can do up here.'

They struggled back towards the cabin. At times Crayfish winced in pain.

Once they were inside, the sound of the storm lessened.

'What do we do now?' said Christopher.

'Wait.'

'Wait for what?'

'Wait for the tide to peak and then subside.'

'What if—'

Crayfish cut him off. 'Don't go thinking the

worst. The last king tide was the highest we've ever had. This one won't be as bad.'

'But—'

'But nothing,' said Crayfish. 'Let's have a cup of tea and then we'll talk.'

Eight

Christopher handed Crayfish a cup of tea.
The weary man nodded his thanks.

'Drink up,' he said. 'There's nothing we can
do but wait. So now, tell me what's on your
mind. Why have you followed me?'

'You've been flirting with my mother,' said Christopher. 'And your wife is still alive.'

'Don't be an idiot,' said Crayfish.

'You told Mum that your wife drowned and her body was never found.'

Crayfish nodded. 'So?'

'So, The Bot said that you visit her every Wednesday. And today is Wednesday.'

Crayfish released a deep sigh and shook his head as if he couldn't believe what he was hearing.

'I only wish she was here,' he said.

Christopher pointed to the dresses in the cupboard.

'They're hers, aren't they?'

Crayfish nodded. 'Yes,' he said.

'Where is she, then?'

'You've got it all wrong,' said Crayfish. 'Your mother is a fine person, but I'm no use to anyone yet.'

'So why are you here?'

'Getting Peggy's things off the boat. Before…'
He didn't seem able to say the words. Instead he waved a hand at the pictures and the candles and the other precious objects.

'I wanted to get her things ashore before…'

'Before the boat goes down,' said Christopher.

'Don't think that,' said Crayfish. His voice began to tremble. 'Look. Peggy drowned. And it was my fault. She got swept overboard. She came to help me get the boat upstream before the king tide hit. I never should have let her. I've been coming here ever since. I just can't forget her. I can't move on.'

Crayfish held his head in his hands.

'I'm sorry,' he said. 'I shouldn't be telling you this. But you've got the wrong idea. I miss her so much. She used to sing while she worked.'

Christopher was no stranger to grief. He had lost a brother and a father. But he didn't know what to say.

Tears began to well in the man's eyes.

'When she died I sort of froze,' he said. 'It ripped my guts out. It fried my brains.'

He pointed to his head. 'I lost all my hair in one week.'

Christopher scratched his own bald head. Their eyes met and, in that moment, something changed. Something was shared.

'Sometimes I have a day when I don't think about my father,' said Christopher.

'Not me,' said Crayfish. 'I'll never get over Peggy. I never have a day like that.'

They continued to talk as the river rose and the storm raged. Christopher's attitude towards Crayfish had changed. But he still felt the need to protect his mother. He didn't want her to fall for a man who still loved someone else. Even if that person was dead.

The boat gave a shudder. Crayfish limped over to the porthole and peered out.

'The river is right up,' he yelled. 'Almost to

the boat.' He threw a life jacket to Christopher. 'Put this on,' he said.

Rolls of thunder shook the forest. The branches outside began to sway and thrash. Lightning flashes lit up the porthole. The boat rose and fell with the branches. The sound of the river below grew louder.

'Look,' said Christopher.

They both stared through the glass. A huge cloud-like wall floated past the porthole.

'Struth,' said Crayfish. 'It's a caravan.' He looked wildly at Christopher. 'Can you swim?'

Christopher smiled proudly. 'I saved Anton when he was drowning in the Atlantic.'

Everything began to tremble. The teacups rattled in protest. The whole vessel suddenly lurched to one side and they were both flung across the floor. The boat began to rock and then suddenly, like a released cork, it lurched upwards and settled.

'We're afloat,' yelled Crayfish. He grabbed

Lonely with one arm and placed the other around Christopher's shoulder. He winced as he put pressure on his injured leg. But despite this and the desperate situation they were in, he tried to add some humour.

'Quick,' he said, giving Lonely's paw a little squeeze. 'All hands on deck.'

Together they made their way out of the cabin. The rain was lashing across the boat. The wind screamed in fury. An unimaginable sight revealed itself. The river was now a swirling lake. Fallen trees and logs spun like floating matchsticks. A half-submerged fishing shack slid by.

The boat was in the middle of it all, rocking from side to side helplessly.

'Can't you start the motor?' said Christopher.

Crayfish shook his head. 'It's in pieces,' he said. 'There's nothing we can do at the moment. It's too dangerous to risk leaving the boat. We'll be okay unless…' He didn't finish the sentence. He stared over the side.

'Unless what?' said Christopher.

'Unless that branch pulls out of the hole.'

Christopher followed his gaze. The branch sticking through the boat had broken away from the tree and was trailing along behind them.

'What if it does?' said Christopher.

'We'll be swept downstream when the tide turns and she'll sink for sure.'

'Can't you drop anchor?' said Christopher.

Crayfish shook his head and said nothing. They both knew it was still sitting on the railway platform.

And then, as suddenly and quickly as it had started, the rain stopped. The sun broke through grey clouds. Now they could see the size of their problem.

'I can't swim with a broken leg,' said Crayfish. 'But even if I could, I can't leave you here. Nor Lonely.'

'I can make it,' said Christopher.

'It's too dangerous,' said Crayfish.

Christopher looked around desperately. 'What about that hatch cover?' he said. 'We could use it as a raft.'

Crayfish nodded. 'That's what it's for,' he said. He looked at his watch. 'But once the tide turns the river will become raging rapids. We'll either be capsized or washed out to sea.' He stared at the broken branch, which was still intact.

But at that very moment there was the sound of a watery explosion.

'The branch has gone,' yelled Crayfish. 'We're sinking.'

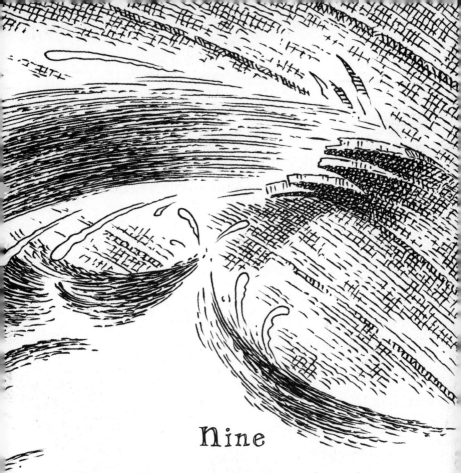

Nine

Christopher rushed to the cabin door and threw it open. The water inside was already ankle-deep. A powerful jet was shooting across the room.

He ran back on deck and stared over the edge. The boat was settling.

'Someone might come,' he said.

They stared at the empty shore and the tree-tops, which seemed to be floating on the surface of the swelling water. The situation was hopeless.

Or was it? What was that? Who was that? He blinked to clear his eyes.

Yes. There, standing in a small clearing, were three figures. Waving.

'Look,' shouted Christopher. 'It's The Bot. And Mum. And Anton.'

Crayfish leapt to his feet excitedly and then screamed. He grasped his left leg. Christopher could see blood seeping through his fingers. Crayfish stood, trembling, his face white, his eyes rolling. Suddenly he collapsed onto the deck. He lay unconscious on his back. Lonely started licking his master's face.

Christopher was torn. He wanted to help Crayfish. But they had to get off the boat or they would drown. The water was now just below deck level.

She was going down. Fast.

He had to hurry.

'Think,' he said. 'Think.' He looked around. A closed locker. What was inside? He ran over to it and threw open the lid. It was full of fishing gear.

'Yes,' he said. He threw the contents aside recklessly until he found what he was looking for – a spool with fishing line wrapped neatly around its core.

'Got it,' he yelled.

He called to Lonely. 'You have to save us,' he said. 'If I swim for it, Crayfish will go down with the boat. And so will you. I know it's dangerous. But you are our only hope.'

Lonely put his head on his paws.

Christopher groaned as a flash of memory shot through his mind. Lonely. Hiding under the train. Refusing to budge.

'Not again,' said Christopher.

He picked up Lonely and carried him to the

edge of the deck. Then he tied the end of the fishing line to the little dog's collar.

'Go,' he said. 'Swim for it, Lonely. Take this line to the shore.'

Lonely sat down and closed his eyes.

'No you don't,' said Christopher. 'I've got something for you to chase.'

The figures on the shore were gesturing desperately with their arms but it was impossible to know what they were trying to say.

He reached into his pocket and pulled out a piece of grease-proof paper.

'Look, look. Look at this,' he shouted.

Lonely opened one eye but wasn't really interested. Until he saw the sausage. Christopher held his arm back behind his head. And threw with all his might.

The sausage sailed through the air in a high arc. Then it began to fall. Lonely was already over the edge before the sausage hit the water, well short of the bank. He began to swim. He was moving sideways, being pulled by the current.

'You can do it, Lonely,' whispered Christopher.

The Bot, Anton and his mother were jumping around and waving. As Christopher watched he saw another person appear there, and then another and another. Every customer the pub had ever had must have been there.

'Go, Lonely, go,' said Christopher. He paid out the line generously.

The head of the little dog was all that could be seen but Christopher knew that under the surface his small legs would be paddling like crazy. It was obvious that Lonely was not going to make it. His legs were tiring. He was being slowly swept upstream.

Suddenly a figure on the shore dashed into the swollen river. It was The Bot. He dived into the rushing water and swam furiously towards Lonely.

'Go, go, go,' said Christopher.

The two heads in the water moved towards each other. And then finally met. The Bot grabbed the little dog and turned over on his back and began to kick his feet.

'Yes,' exclaimed Christopher.

The crowd was pulling on a rope that had been tied to The Bot. For what seemed like hours, he moved closer to the shore. Finally, he stood and held the dog high in the air for all to see.

'They've got it,' shouted Christopher. 'They've got it. Well done, Lonely.'

There was a tug on the fishing line and more waving. Christopher started to wind it back in, immediately feeling the pull of the rope on the other end. As he heaved, the weight on the line increased.

'Don't break, don't break,' he said.

He snatched a glance at Crayfish, who was still flat on his back with his eyes closed.

The water had now risen and covered the portholes. At any moment it would be sweeping the deck. Christopher dropped the spool and began pulling on the line, hand over hand, dropping the cord behind him in tangled coils.

'Got it,' he yelled as the end of the thick rope slipped over the railing. He bit off the fishing line and rushed to the hatch cover. With trembling fingers, he tied the rope to one of its steel rings. Water swirled around his feet and covered the sagging canvas that protected the hold.

He grabbed Crayfish under the arms and dragged him onto the floating hatch cover. Just in time. The boat began to tilt sideways. Its port-side railing disappeared under the water. On the starboard side the railing was now high in the air.

Their raft shivered and began to slide over the submerged rail into the water. Christopher threw himself across Crayfish's prone body to pin him down. He desperately grabbed the edge of the hatch cover.

With a gurgle the front edge of the hatch cover plunged into the swirling water.

Christopher closed his eyes and held his breath as he and Crayfish were sucked beneath the surface.

For a frozen second they remained tilted, with one end of the cover below the surface and the other reaching for the sky. Then it corrected.

With an enormous thump the raised half whacked back onto the surface.

Christopher gasped for air. He choked and spluttered. For a moment he fought to understand what had happened. Then he realised. Their raft was floating. And they were both still alive.

But far from safe. He waved in panic at the far-off figures.

'Pull,' he screamed. 'Pull.'

They were drifting sideways. But then the rope tightened and they began to move slowly towards the shore. A long line of people on the edge of the river were pulling like contestants in a tug of war.

Crayfish groaned and gave a small cough, but his eyes were still closed.

'Hurry, hurry,' shouted Christopher. He began pulling on the rope himself but had to release his grip as it slipped through his fingers, ripping at the skin.

But there was hope. He could see that the raft was moving closer and closer to the bank. The seconds seemed like days. And the minutes like weeks. But in the end he felt a bump as the raft hit the shore. He jumped off and staggered onto the wet grass.

He felt his mother's embracing arms.

'Christopher, oh, Christopher,' she gasped.

He hugged her weakly.

'Crayfish,' he mumbled.

A small crowd was surrounding the prone figure. A cheer went up as Crayfish opened his eyes, sat up and groaned. He was blinking in confusion.

He stared at the hatch cover and the rope and the faces looking down at him.

'Who did it?' he said. 'Who saved us?'

The Bot pointed to Lonely and then to Christopher.

'Christopher did,' he said. 'He's a hero.'

Christopher clapped a hand on The Bot's back. 'This man is a wonder,' he said. 'He's the true hero.'

'It wasn't just me,' The Bot said shyly. 'It was everyone. Out here in the bush we all...' He stared at the rope and grinned. 'Pull together.'

The others smiled but then everyone fell silent as they saw Crayfish staring out at his boat.

Only the starboard railing and part of the bridge could be seen as the dying vessel tipped further onto its side. Suddenly it rolled right over. Bottom up.

Then it tipped lengthwise with its propeller pointing at the heavens. The whole vessel shuddered and began to slip forwards into the gurgling water. Christopher could see the name of the boat painted on its stern. He couldn't quite make it out. The writing was upside down.

'*PEGGY*,' said Anton.

The boat trembled and then disappeared. A burst of bubbles briefly marked its watery grave.

A single tear trickled down Crayfish's cheek.

'She's gone,' he said. No one spoke.

Christopher stared at Crayfish. Was he talking about the boat? Or the woman he had married and loved for so many years?

Pat put a hand on Crayfish's shoulder and then hugged him. 'Gone,' she said. 'But not forgotten.'

Christopher smiled. He knew that the man was freed from the ghosts of his past.

And so was he. He saw his mother comfort the grieving man and the concern on the faces of his friends. In that moment he realised that this land and these people had something to offer that he had thought only existed in the past.

'Hey, you two,' he said. 'Let's go home.'

Ten

Six months later, Christopher was in the bedroom twiddling the dials on his radio transmitter. He looked out the window and saw the others sitting outside the pub. They were under a sun umbrella at one of the tables that were scattered around on the grass.

'Time for lunch,' he said. He took off his headphones and left the room.

The winter sun shone on his back with just the right amount of warmth. As he made his way to their table, he couldn't help but reflect on the changes the pub had undergone.

A group of tourists who had escaped from the cold southern states filled up most of the outside tables. More were eating inside.

The new toilet and shower block glistened under a fresh coat of paint.

Christopher glanced at the sign hanging over the glass doors and the windows with flywire screens, Pat's idea. He read the new name of the pub to himself and smiled.

Pat, Crayfish and Anton looked up as he arrived.

'Hey, guess what,' said Christopher. 'I've just been on the School of the Air. Anton got an A for English.'

'Congratulations, Anton,' said Pat.

He gave a shy smile in return.

'What's the teacher's name?' said Crayfish.

'Rabbit,' said Christopher.

'And what do they call you?' said Crayfish.

Christopher blushed.

'Long Drop,' yelled Anton. 'Everyone calls him Long Drop.'

Pat tried not to laugh but she couldn't help herself.

'Don't laugh,' said Christopher with a grin. 'Or I'll think of a worse nickname for you.'

A Different Dog

'Short, spare in its telling and yet with incredible breadth
of subjects – memory, loss, friendship, trauma and resilience –
it's a book which, like a concertina, expands out to occupy
every corner of the mind, leaving readers thinking, feeling
and left feeling that little bit more alive after reading.
It's a triumph!' – *Jake Hope, Youth Libraries Group
and Reading Consultant*

'A tale of empathy, love, loss and friendship. A future classic
and compact story which will make your heart beat a little
faster and your eyes a lot wetter. Superb!' – *@BookMonsterAlly*

'Full of quiet, resilience and graceful lyricism, Jennings'
humour peeks in at the end, gloriously.' – *@librarymice*

'A moving and powerful read for those looking for something
a bit different.' – *North Somerset Teacher's Book Award blog*

'Compelling and tersely written – every word counts –
this is a book to hold you in its thrall even after you've
put it aside. Geoff Kelly's black and white illustrations are
atmospheric and powerful.' – *Red Reading Hub review*

A Different Dog

Paul

JENNINGS

A Different Boy

Longlisted for the CILIP Carnegie Medal 2019

'This perfect jewel of a novella explores loss,
isolation and the difficult migrant experience with spare,
eloquent prose.' – *Alison Brumwell, Chair of CILIP
Carnegie Medal judges 2019*

'Like all books by Paul Jennings, this one... draws you in
immediately and grips you throughout. Like the author's
previous titles too, it's superbly written without a wasted word.
Having said that, it's also quite unlike any of his previous
titles.' – *Red Reading Hub review*

'*A Different Boy*' is a gripping read and the twist in the middle
will leave readers gasping.' – *Sydney Morning Herald*

Visit the Old Barn Books website to watch Paul Jennings
reading from *A Different Boy* and hear his responses to the
interview questions put to him by Alison Brumwell for the
Youth Libraries Group conference.

A Different Boy

Paul
JENNINGS

Paul Jennings has written over one hundred stories and has won every Australian children's choice book award. Since the publication of *Unreal!* in 1985, readers all around the world have loved his books. The top-rating TV series *Round the Twist* was based on a selection of his enormously popular short story collections, such as *Unseen!*. In 1995, Jennings was made a Member of the Order of Australia for services to children's literature and he was awarded the prestigious Dromkeen Medal in 2001. In 2019, *A Different Boy* was longlisted for the Carnegie Medal in the UK and Jennings received a Lifetime Achievement Award from the Children's Book Council of Australia.

Much of Paul Jennings' writing draws on his childhood experience of emigrating to Australia from England and his subsequent career working as a teacher and speech therapist. Teacher's notes for the titles published by Old Barn Books are available from our website.

www.pauljennings.com